IF YO...   ...TO
SCARE
YOURSELF

IF YOU WANT TO SCARE YOURSELF

YOURSELF

Angela Sommer-Bodenburg

Interior illustrations by Helga Spiess

Translated from the German
by Renée Vera Cafiero

SCHOLASTIC INC.
New York Toronto London Auckland Sydney

ISBN 0-590-43830-1

12 11 10 9 8 7 6 5 4 3 2 1   0 1 2 3 4 5/9

Printed in the U.S.A.   42

First Scholastic printing, October 1990

CONTENTS

BARBARA

Freddy was sick. He had been sick for two long weeks. He had an infected leg that wasn't healing quickly, and he had to stay in bed. The wound burned and itched, and whenever his mother changed the bandage, it hurt terribly. But the boredom was even worse than the pain. He was the most bored in the mornings, after his parents had gone off to work.

Often he just lay around and counted the black dots on the wallpaper. Or he made up his own stories, about a boy and his dog doing exciting things together.

When his mother came home at noon, she was almost always too tired to bother with him.

That's the way it was today.

After lunch Freddy asked, "Are you going to play with me?" but his mother just shook her head.

Freddy gave her a black look. "Being sick is awful!"

"Well, I'd be happy to stay in bed for a week and let myself get spoiled," his mother replied.

"Spoiled?" Freddy almost laughed. "I'm alone all morning. And when you do finally get home, you never have time for me. You could pay more attention to me, you know!"

"I've had a very tiring morning," she said.

Freddy bit his lips. "Even so."

"What if I sat by your bed later and told you a story?"

"Just one story?"

"A scary story!"

"You know a scary story?" Freddy asked, surprised.

"Not only do I know one, it's one that happened to me."

"Oh, yes—tell it!"

"Later—when I've read the paper and made coffee."

"Did this scary story really happen to you?" asked Freddy, his eyes shining, when his mother finally sat down next to his bed.

"Yes."

"Had I been born yet?"

"It was two years ago, when we were looking for an apartment. Before we found this one, we almost rented a four-room apartment in an old house with a big weed-grown garden."

"And why didn't you take it?"

"That's what I'm going to tell you."

Daddy had found the ad in the paper. The rent was very reasonable, so we arranged to see the place.

The house looked like a small castle—it even had a little turret. I was very taken with it. You know how I like old houses! And I liked the garden, with its big old trees. So I went up to the second floor and rang the bell.

I waited awhile. Finally I heard footsteps, and a little girl opened the door. She had curly, black hair that hung down to her waist, and she was wearing a long, white, lace dress. Her face was very pale.

"You're here to see the apartment?" she asked politely.

"Yes," I said. "Are your parents home?"

"They'll be right here," she said. "But I can show you around. Please come in."

I went in.

The girl stared at me and asked, "Do you have children?"

"Yes. A boy."

"And what's his name?"

"Freddy."

The girl smiled for the first time.

"My name is Barbara," she said. "Come on, I'll show you Freddy's room."

"But I'd rather see the other rooms first," I objected.

"No, no," Barbara said quickly. "You have to see Freddy's room first."

Her voice sounded so insistent that I followed her. She led me to a large, empty room at the end of the hall. The brightly colored wallpaper made me guess that it had once been a child's room.

Barbara ran to the window.

"This is where my table was," she said. "I could always see the chestnut tree when I sat

here. Your son has to sit by the window too—promise me that?"

"I don't know," I answered uncertainly, and I tried to laugh.

"Please!" she said, and looked at me with huge, imploring eyes.

"All right, if you insist," I said, just to humor her. Of course, I was really thinking that it would be our own business how we would arrange the rooms.

"And that's where my bed was!" She pointed at the wall next to the window. "When I woke up in the morning, I could see the sky. So I always knew whether the weather was nice or not."

"But that's not a good place for a bed," I said.

She looked at me in surprise. "Why not?"

"There's often a draft by a window. You could have caught cold."

10

"Caught cold?" she cried. "Are you s̲a̲y̲[...] that my mother didn't take good care of me?"

"Of course not," I hastened to reassure her.

"But you said it wasn't a good place for a bed!"

"I was just making conversation."

"Don't ever say such a terrible thing about my mother!" Her voice suddenly took on a sharp edge.

"But I didn't say anything about your mother," I said—and then I heard voices in the hallway.

"That must be your parents!" I said, relieved. I left the room quickly. I knew it was silly, but I found the little girl eerie.

In the hallway a woman and a man came toward me. At first I was startled, because they were both dressed all in black. The man had the same black hair as Barbara, the woman the same large eyes.

"You're already here?" the woman asked, astonished.

"How odd—I thought I had locked the front door," said the man.

I wanted to explain that their daughter had opened the door for me, but before I could say anything, they went into one of the front rooms. Then they began to show me around. They showed me the two living rooms, the bedroom, and finally the bath-room.

We stopped in the kitchen, which had beautiful old tiles. The man turned his face—it was almost as pale as Barbara's—to me and asked, "Do you like the apartment?"

"Yes," I said enthusiastically. "It's a little old-fashioned, just what I wanted. And it's very spacious."

"There's another room," said the man, "at the end of the hall. But we don't go in there anymore."

"It was our daughter's room," his wife added quietly.

"I know," I said—surprised that they were so shy about mentioning that empty room.

"You—" The woman hesitated. "You've seen the room?"

"Yes—your daughter showed it to me."

The woman stared at me. "Our daughter?"

"Yes." I nodded. "She wanted me to arrange the room exactly the way she had it."

"What did she look like?" cried the man hoarsely.

I was surprised by the question.

"She had long, black hair and was wearing a white, lace dress."

"Barbara!" cried the woman. Her voice was so full of pain that I was a little frightened.

Then they both ran out of the kitchen and down the hall calling Barbara's name.

I felt more and more uneasy. I didn't understand why they were so excited, but it seemed clear that my talk with Barbara had upset them.

Slowly I followed them.

They stood at the door of Barbara's room.

"She's not here," said the man dully.

"But I saw her," I assured them. "She was standing over there by the window, talking about her chestnut tree."

The woman shook her head sadly. "You must be mistaken."

"I'm sure I'm not."

"You are. It's impossible."

"But why?"

"Barbara is dead," said the man.

"Dead?" I repeated in disbelief.

"She died four weeks ago," the man explained, "here in this room, of pneumonia."

"No!" I cried.

The woman and the man looked at me and nodded.

I turned and ran away.

Freddy's mother paused.

Then she added, "A week later we found this apartment here, and were we glad that no ghost opened the door when we rang the bell."

"Did Barbara look like a ghost?" Freddy wanted to know.

"She was very pale and very delicate—like someone who has been sick for a long time."

"Why didn't you take me with you?"

"You were in school, that's why. And now I have to go." She stood up. "I still have a lot to do."

Freddy made a face, but he didn't say anything.

He heard her go into the kitchen, and then there was the clattering of dishes.

"Mom?" he called.

"What is it?"

"Did Barbara die because her bed was too close to the window?"

"I don't know."

"Is it true that her mother didn't take good care of her?"

"I don't know!"

Freddy took a deep breath and called, "I could get pneumonia too, if you don't pay more attention to me."

His mother didn't answer.

Freddy closed his eyes and sighed.

HARRY

Usually at six o'clock Freddy's father came home.

"Dad, do you know a scary story?"

"Do I know what?"

"A scary story," said Freddy. "Did one ever happen to you?"

"One happens to me every day," his father answered. "It's about a man who comes home tired and has to tell stories."

"You're mean! You think it's fun for me to hang around in bed all the time!"

"No, I don't think that." His father looked at Freddy's leg. "Has it gotten better yet?"

"Yes," Freddy said. "It's just the boredom that's getting worse."

"Okay. Maybe I'll tell you a story after dinner."

"A scary story?"

"If you want to scare yourself—okay then, you'll hear my story about Harry!"

After dinner his father sat next to Freddy's bed and began to tell the story: "It happened when I was in seventh grade. I was so bad in math that I was going to be left back a year.

"One day a new boy came into class, Harry Ackerman. He was very different from us, and no one liked him."

"What do you mean—different?" asked Freddy.

Well, Harry didn't seem to care one bit about how he looked. He always wore the same black shirt and the same black pants. His hair was down to his collar and looked as if he'd never washed it, and his face was an unhealthy, pale color. And he smelled so peculiar that no one wanted to sit next to

him—except when we had a math test. Because in math Harry was the best. He could even stump the teacher with his questions.

Of course, Harry soon noticed that I didn't have the foggiest idea about math. So a couple of times he suggested that he would be glad to tutor me—and he didn't even want to be paid for it.

I turned his offer down every time—something inside me kept telling me to say no. But one day when an exceptionally hard assignment was due, I let myself be talked into studying with him.

"You won't regret it!" Harry said in a rough voice.

"Where shall we meet?" I asked him. "At your house?"

"No," he said quickly, "my place is no good. But what about at your place? Do you have your own room?"

I nodded.

"And do your parents leave you home alone sometimes?"

"Yes—my mother cleans people's houses in the afternoons. But why do you want us to be alone?"

"Why?" He gave a hoarse laugh. "Because we won't be distracted then!"

That seemed reasonable enough at the time—although I didn't find the idea of being alone in the apartment with Harry especially appealing.

But then, I told myself, Harry was just a classmate, a boy my own age, and I arranged to meet him that afternoon. At four o'clock my mother left the apartment, and right afterward the doorbell rang.

Harry stood in the doorway, a half hour early. I suspected he had been watching from the stairwell, but I didn't say anything.

We went to my room. I noticed that the unpleasant smell coming from Harry had gotten stronger. I suddenly felt as if I couldn't breathe, and I yanked the window open.

Harry watched me.

"Is something wrong?" he asked.

"No, no," I said quickly, and sat down.

We opened our books, and Harry began to explain the math problems to me. After we had worked for an hour, Harry said that that was enough for one day. He was right: I was so exhausted, I was falling asleep over my notebooks.

When I opened my eyes, Harry had disappeared. I looked at my watch: It was a little past six, and I could hear my mother coming home.

The next day in school I was still tired—but when it was my turn at the blackboard,

I was able to figure out the math problem that Harry had explained to me.

That afternoon Harry and I studied together again.

We sat beside each other at the big table in my room and did more problems. This time I hardly noticed Harry's unique aroma, and I had also gotten used to his strange, hypnotic voice.

Harry was an excellent tutor. For the first time I felt that math might be a subject I could learn after all.

We made more progress than the day before, but once again I fell asleep. Harry was gone when I woke up. I happened to look at my math notebook, and there, right under the last problem we did, were two little spots of blood. I checked my hands, but I couldn't find any cuts.

The next day we had a quiz. I managed to

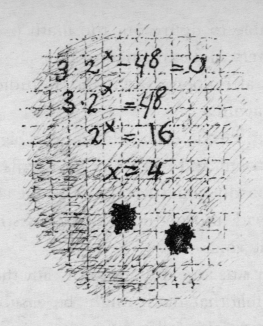

$$3 \cdot 2^x - 48 = 0$$
$$3 \cdot 2^x = 48$$
$$2^x = 16$$
$$x = 4$$

solve more than half the problems.

I got a C—my first passing grade in many months.

Harry praised me, but at the same time he insisted that we must not stop my lessons or I'd forget everything.

So we continued to meet in my room every afternoon.

28

And every afternoon after my lesson, I would fall asleep. It was embarrassing, but it didn't seem to make any difference to Harry—at least he never mentioned it.

I got better and better at math. Our math teacher, who had practically given up on me, thought it was a miracle. He didn't know that Harry was tutoring me, and neither did my classmates.

I didn't tell anyone. Not even my mother knew I had a visitor every afternoon. She only noticed that I was suddenly getting good marks in math—and that I was always tired.

Soon I even started to fall asleep at the dinner table. My head would simply fall forward, and I would wake up when my mother would shake me by the shoulder and ask anxiously whether I was sick.

Finally she insisted on taking me to the doctor. He said I had a severe case of anemia and prescribed some pills for me. From then on I took three pills a day.

Nevertheless I was still tired all the time. It got so bad that I had to spend a week at home in bed.

Harry never came to see me that week. Maybe he had found out that my mother had taken a leave of absence from work and was staying home all day.

Within the week I recovered so much that even the doctor was surprised.

When I went back to school, I was told that Harry had been absent for the last two days too. No one knew whether he was sick. I decided to drop in on him that afternoon.

Our teacher gave me his address.

Harry lived on a street at the other end of town. On the way there I kept wondering why Harry was going to our school if he lived so far away.

Finally I got to the street our teacher had said was Harry's.

It was a narrow and dark street. On either side stood large, gray blocks of apartment buildings. It all seemed so oppressive that I felt like running away.

Harry lived in the second-to-last block. It was a building like all the rest. The plaster was crumbling, and the paint had flaked from the window frames.

The front door of the building looked old and decayed, and the board that held the buzzers was full of worm holes. I tried to read the names on the faded labels. I couldn't find Ackerman, but two of the labels were illegible.

I would just have to climb the stairs from floor to floor to find Harry's apartment. I opened the door and found myself in a long, dark corridor.

In the dim light that came through the dirty panes of the front door, I saw something large and black. My heart began to beat rapidly. I turned on the light switch and was relieved to find it was a moped that someone had left next to the cellar door.

I walked on, but I couldn't find the name Ackerman on any door on the first and second floors.

So I climbed the rickety stairs that rattled and creaked with every step, up to the top floor. WIELAND, it said on the left door, F. STEIN on the right one.

After a moment's hesitation I rang the STEIN bell. A young woman with a baby in her arms opened the door. She looked at me suspiciously.

"I'm trying to visit a classmate," I said, embarrassed.

"Yes, so?" she asked unkindly.

"His name is Harry. Harry Ackerman."

"Don't know him."

"But he's supposed to live in this building," I said.

She shrugged her shoulders. "Go ask the Wielands—they've been living here for thirty years. We just moved in six months ago." Without another word she slammed the door shut.

So I rang the WIELAND bell.

After a while I heard shuffling foot-steps.

"Who's there?" asked a voice behind the door.

"I'm looking for a classmate," I answered. "Harry Ackerman."

The door opened, and I saw an old man. An unusually large, pitch-black cat wove around his legs.

"They don't live here anymore," he said.

35

"But our teacher gave me this address," I replied.

"Harry Ackerman . . ." the man spat out. It sounded as if he didn't think very highly of Harry. "His poor mother, his poor little sister!"

I started to get goose bumps.

"Tell me what happened to them," I said.

"Gone," he said tonelessly, "all gone."

"How do you mean?"

"They both got sick . . . chlorosis!"

"Chlorosis?" I repeated, at a loss.

"First his mother had it. She got weaker and weaker, until it was too late. Then his sister got it, and it wasn't two weeks before she was dead."

"Dead?"

"Yes."

Suddenly I felt sorry for Harry. I had never guessed that he was having problems at home!

"Was Harry sick too?"

The old man laughed bitterly. "Not him! On the contrary—*he* got stronger every day. He seemed to be thriving. Some of us here in the building even thought—" He broke off and added in a whisper, "Some of us thought he had something to do with his mother's and sister's illnesses. . . ."

"How could . . . ?"

"Anyway, Harry disappeared the day his sister died."

"He disappeared?" I asked, astonished.

"Yes. I haven't seen Harry since then."

"But—He's in my class!"

The old man looked at me and smiled mockingly. "How old are you?"

"Fifteen."

"Is that so? Harry Ackerman would have to be at least forty by now. Everything I've just told you happened twenty-five years ago."

"That's impossible!" I cried—then I stopped. For just as the pieces of a jigsaw puzzle eventually fit together to make a picture, my mind suddenly formed a terrible, completely unbelievable image: Harry's old-fashioned clothing, his unpleasant odor, my instinctive distrust of him, the deep sleep I fell into each time we studied together, my

constant tiredness, the spots of blood in my notebook, the doctor's diagnosis . . .

"What—what is chlorosis?" I asked.

"Another word for anemia," he answered.

I saw the old man as if through a fog. He asked me something, but I didn't understand him. There was a roaring in my ears, and I thought I was going to faint. I turned around and went down the stairs, my legs shaking the whole way.

When I got home, my mother put me to bed right away and blamed herself loudly for having let me go out at all.

I never did see Harry again—and I also never again had anemia. . . .

Freddy's father finished the story.

"Did you like that one?" he asked.

"Yes!" said Freddy. "But did all that really happen to you?"

His father smiled. "You wanted to hear a scary story, and I've told you one."

Freddy tried to figure out how to worm the truth out of his father.

"Were you really going to be left back?

Mom always says you're good at math."

"Because Harry explained it all to me!"

"So there really was a Harry?"

"Of course."

"And—Was he a vampire?"

"Maybe. . . . Anyway, I managed to pass math after all, and that was the main thing as far as I was concerned," Freddy's father answered, and got up.

"Tell me another scary story," Freddy begged. "Just one more!"

"Make one up yourself!"

"If it were that simple . . ."

THE CHILD
UNDER
THE CLOAK

As she had promised, Freddy's grandmother came the next day.

"You're still not allowed to get up?" she asked.

"No," said Freddy curtly.

"Does it still hurt?"

"Yes."

"You *could* be a little more talkative."

"Oh, Grandma! I really don't feel like talking about my dumb leg all the time!"

"And what would you like to talk about?" asked his grandmother, offended.

"About Dad. Was he always good at math?"

"Not especially."

"Did he ever have a tutor?"

"No. We couldn't have afforded it."

"But there are people who will do it and

don't get paid for it."

"Really? Who do you mean?" his grandmother asked doubtfully.

"Harry, for example," answered Freddy,
and looked at Grandma to see whether she
would react to Harry's name.

"Harry?" she asked. "Is that a boy in your
class? Does he want to tutor you?"

"Me? Oh, no!" cried Freddy, alarmed.

"But you must have missed a lot of school-
work," she said. "It wouldn't hurt a bit if
Harry helped you. Especially if it's free."

"I don't want to have anything to do with
Harry!" Freddy yelled—louder than he
really meant to.

Right away Grandma noticed something
was up. "Why? What's the matter with him?"
she asked.

"Oh, nothing," mumbled Freddy. "He's
only . . . a little funny."

"Just like you!" said Grandma.

"I'm not funny!" Freddy protested. "I'm just sick and bored. And so you have to tell me a scary story!"

"A scary story?" Grandma grinned, amused. "I never knew you were interested in those. Scary stories are old-fashioned, you know."

"That's just what's nice about them!"

"All right. . . . Then I'll tell you a scary story!"

It was on a Monday. Shortly before it was time for the shops to close, I noticed that I didn't have any bread and cold cuts in the house for my supper.

I quickly put on a jacket and went out.

It was colder and windier outside than I had thought. But I didn't want to go back. I raised my collar and quickly walked on. At the corner I almost bumped into a child

hopping over the cracks in the sidewalk.

Angrily I stepped aside. "Why don't you look out!" I said.

The child looked at me with a strange smile. Its face was ashen, and there were dark shadows under its eyes.

There was something about the child that alarmed me, but I couldn't figure out what it was. Nor could I see much more than its face, for the child was wearing a dirty yellow cloak. It had a hood that was much too large pulled over its head. I couldn't even tell if it was a boy or a girl. Then the child began to hop again, and I suddenly saw that it was barefoot—on an October day!

"Don't you have any shoes?" I asked, shocked.

No answer—just a smile. I thought the child might have its shoes hidden under the cloak, to make a fool of me.

"Answer me, do you have shoes?" I cried.

A shake of the head.

"But it's much too cold to go around bare-foot!"

Another smile.

"Do you hear me?" I said. "It's too cold. You'll catch cold. You'll get a fever. You could catch your death!"

"Are you saying you're worried about me?" asked the child. It looked at me attentively, as if my answer were very important.

"Why, if you're barefoot, I have to be worried about you," I replied.

"You're worried—about me!" the child said happily.

A shudder ran down my back. Hastily I said, "I have to go now. The stores are about to close."

"You're going? Now? After all that?" asked the child.

There was almost a challenge in the way

the child spoke those words, so I asked, "What do you mean?"

The child answered calmly, "You said you were worried about me. That means you'll never let me down."

I tried to laugh. "I can't let you down anyway. I hardly know you."

"But now we know each other!" the child answered. "And that's why you have to take me home with you."

Such boldness left me speechless for a moment. Then I said, "Take you with me? Go home to your own parents!"

"I have no parents," the child answered. Dark eyes looked at me pleadingly. "Please take me with you."

"You must have taken leave of your senses," I said angrily, and turned to go.

The child grabbed my arm and begged, "Let me go with you!"

"No!" I said, and brushed its clinging hand

away from me. Then I hurried off, not bothering to turn around.

It was only when I reached the bakery that I looked back—and I saw the child in the same place, lying on the sidewalk.

I suddenly felt sorry that I had pushed the poor child away and, feeling guilty, I ran back. The child lay there like a wilted yellow flower, completely covered by the cloak.

"Are you hurt?" I asked, worried.

There was no answer.

"Oh, please get up!" I said.

Still no answer.

"If you want, I'll give you some hot chocolate at my house," I said temptingly.

Silence.

"Do you want a shove?" I joked.

When there was still no reply, I lifted the cloak—and froze: There was nothing under it!

A woman came out of a nearby shop. "Are you a relative?" she asked.

I didn't understand her question. "A relative? Whose?"

"The child's—the one who was run over, here, an hour ago. Wearing this cloak. I'm sure you'll want to take it with you."

I was too confused to reply. Numbly I snatched up the cloak; it nestled against me like a child's body, and I ran home.

"Do you still have the cloak?" asked Freddy.

"Oh, no. I washed it and donated it to a clothing drive."

"Was it true that the child had been run over?"

"I wasn't there. . . ."

"But I want to know!"

"With a scary story you can't ask about the how and why," Grandma answered, "or it loses its magic."

WOLFGANG

After Freddy's grand-
mother had left, his
mother came home
from work.

"Did you have a nice
morning together?" she
asked.

"Grandma told me a
scary story," Freddy answered.

"So you certainly weren't bored!"

"No. But now I'm bored again."

"If the scary stories aren't getting to be too
much for you, I'll tell you another one later.
I thought of it on the way home."

"I never get tired of scary stories."

She laughed. "Okay. But you have to be
patient a little longer."

"Until you've had time to read the paper
and make coffee. I know," said Freddy.

When his mother's coffee was ready, she

came into Freddy's room with her cup.

"This happened when I was about as old as you," she began her story. "My mother got very sick. She was in the hospital for several weeks."

"What was wrong with her?" asked Freddy. "Did she have an infected leg, like me?"

No. She had to have a stomach operation. And, of course, all this *had* to happen just at the beginning of summer vacation, when she had planned to take me on a trip. Naturally we didn't go. Instead she sent me to her sister, Aunt Matilda, who had been working for some time as a governess for a rich family in the country. I had to get there all by myself, and when I arrived at the train station, Aunt Matilda wasn't even there to pick me up.

I wanted to take the next train and go back home!

Instead I asked for directions and walked up the road a short distance.

Finally I saw the big white house in front of me, just as the stationmaster had described it. It was an old manor house, with columns on either side of the main entrance. The gate was open, and I went through the front garden to the entrance.

I pressed the buzzer timidly.

No one came to the door.

Wasn't Aunt Matilda at home?

I thought about the letter she had written me. I knew it by heart because it was so eerie:

Dear Sabina, she had written, *of course you can come and stay with me during your vacation.*

It's just that you mustn't be surprised at the people here—they're somewhat unusual. But you're a brave girl, aren't you?

I can't wait to see you!

Your Aunt Matilda

I rang again.

This time the door opened. A man stood there dressed like a butler in an old movie, in a black suit, a black bow tie—and white gloves!

I was speechless.

"Can I help you?" he asked.

"I—I'm Sabina," I stammered.

His expression didn't change. "And what

is your business?"

"I came to visit my aunt—Aunt Matilda. She works here."

To my great relief he smiled a little. "Oh, yes," he said. "She forgot you in all the excitement. Come in. Your aunt is still busy, but she'll come down and greet you right away."

He led me into a great hall and asked me to wait.

I sat down and looked around.

The hall was so big and so high, I felt as if I were in a church—only here there were heavy carpets on the floor, and instead of pictures of saints, old paintings of hunting scenes and family portraits hung on the walls. It was also as quiet and solemn as a church—until I heard the scream, which was followed by sounds of knocking and tumbling.

Then silence again.

Suddenly I was afraid—of the house, of its family, and of the butler, whom I heard coughing softly in the next room.

At that moment my aunt came down the broad stairs. I ran to her and hugged her.

"Why, Sabina, you're trembling!" she said.

"I—I heard a scream," I stammered. "It sounded as if someone was being murdered."

My aunt didn't seem one bit frightened. "Let's go up to my room" was all she said.

Still confused, I followed her.

We went through several rooms, until we reached her little apartment—two rooms, a kitchen, and a bath.

I recognized Aunt Matilda's old red sofa, her bookcase, her floor lamp, and the round table.

We sat on the sofa. "You must be wondering why I didn't come to pick you up," Aunt Matilda said.

I nodded.

"Of course I wanted to be at the train station when you arrived," she explained. "But my pupil, Wolfgang, ran into the garden, and we all had to search for him. It was very difficult, because the garden in the back is a maze. Do you know what a maze is?"

"Not exactly."

"It's a garden with many confusing paths and high hedges. It's very hard to find your way out."

"There's something like that here?" I asked, startled.

"Our maze is a hundred years old," said Aunt Matilda. She sounded as if she were proud of it. "It's very big. You must never go into it alone. Do you promise me?"

"Yes," I agreed readily.

"If your mother hadn't had to go to the hospital, I would never have invited you here," she continued. "The people in this house are peculiar. Especially Wolfgang, the boy. He's sick."

"Does he need an operation?" I asked, thinking of my mother.

"No," answered Aunt Matilda. "He's not sick in that way—let's see, how can I explain it to you?" She hesitated. Then she said, "Well, you'll see him at dinner."

"Aren't we eating here, in your kitchen?" After what Aunt Matilda had told me about the people who lived in the house, I would have preferred to be alone with her.

"No, today we're invited to have dinner with them. Maybe they want Wolfgang to make friends with you."

I don't want to make friends with him, I thought. But I didn't say anything.

I remembered the scream that I had heard, and I asked, "Was that Wolfgang screaming?"

"Yes," my aunt said.

"Why?"

"His father wanted to cut his nails."

"That's why he screamed?" I almost laughed out loud. He must be a funny boy, if he screamed at the top of his lungs just because someone wanted to cut his nails!

But at least I wasn't afraid of him anymore; instead I looked forward to dinner and seeing for myself what Wolfgang was like.

At first when we went into the dining room, I was almost blinded. There were mirrors all over the walls, and there was a lamp in front of every mirror.

A huge chandelier hung from the ceiling, and on the long table, set as if for a feast, gold and silver seemed to flash like lightning.

It was like a fairy-tale movie.

Even the three people who sat at the table could have been in a movie.

The fat man in the navy-blue suit, who had

only a sparse crown of hair left on the back of his head, was certainly twice as old as the thin, blond woman in the low-cut red dress who was sitting next to him. But the most remarkable person was Wolfgang: He had a narrow face and thick, unkempt hair. His heavy eyebrows met over his nose. There was something about him that was wild, untamed, something that didn't fit at all into these elegant surroundings.

"My niece Sabina," Aunt Matilda introduced me. "And this is Wolfgang."

He raised his head and studied me. His eyes were bright yellow—a color I had never seen a person have before.

Uneasily I offered Wolfgang my hand, and was startled by his strong handshake. His hand felt rough and hard, and his nails dug painfully into the back of my hand.

"P-pleased to meet you," I stuttered,

because nothing better occurred to me to say.

Wolfgang growled something I didn't catch. It didn't sound very friendly.

Then dinner was served by a young woman in a white apron and cap. First there was soup. Since no one spoke, I could hear clearly the way Wolfgang slurped his soup from the spoon. His mother looked at him with disapproval several times, but it didn't seem to bother him.

Next there were baked potatoes, carrots, and steaks.

I watched Wolfgang staring at the steaks. He seemed ravenous. His mouth was half open, and I saw a row of sharp white teeth.

While we were eating, I noticed that Wolfgang didn't use a knife and fork. Instead he just speared the meat on his fork, then tore it off with his sharp teeth.

"Eat properly! Chew right!" his mother ordered. But Wolfgang didn't pay any attention.

After finishing his first steak, he quickly grabbed another one from the tray with his fingers.

"Wolfgang, use the silverware!" his mother snapped.

"What will Sabina think of you?" his father added.

Wolfgang didn't answer.

He gobbled the meat and stretched out his

hand for yet another piece.

"That's enough!" his mother cried.

"I'm hungry!" said Wolfgang in a rough, throaty voice.

"Then eat vegetables and potatoes!"

"But I want meat!"

"No!" His mother quickly pulled the tray with the last two steaks toward her.

"If I let you cut my nails, will I get more meat?" Now Wolfgang's voice sounded soft, ingratiating. His parents exchanged a glance.

"All right," said his mother, "one piece, but

only if you promise."

"Only one?" Wolfgang exploded. "I want *both* of them!"

"Then comb your hair!" said his father.

"No!" Wolfgang jumped up so suddenly that he knocked his chair over. Then he ran to the door and slammed it behind him.

"Shouldn't we go after him?" asked my aunt.

Wolfgang's father shook his head. "It's better if we leave him alone until he comes to his senses."

We spent the rest of the meal in silence. Reluctantly I ate everything on my plate. My appetite had disappeared, and I also didn't understand what Wolfgang found so special about the steaks: They weren't even cooked well—they were dripping with blood!

After dinner Aunt Matilda and I went to her apartment.

"Are you going to show me the maze now?" I asked.

"I'd rather not," she said.

"But it's still light out."

"The doors are all locked now," she said, and then added, "In this house even the windows have locks."

"Are they afraid of burglars?"

"No. It's Wolfgang. He's moonstruck."

"Moonstruck?" I asked, astonished.

"Yes. Whenever the moon is full, like today, he goes through a strange transformation. He doesn't want to take a bath, comb his hair, or eat anything—except meat. His parents think he does it on purpose, to get them angry. That's why they are so harsh with him."

"Wolfgang looks very different from his parents," I said.

"He's the son from his father's first marriage," Aunt Matilda explained. "The young blond woman is his stepmother. Wolfgang's father married her two years ago. And apparently Wolfgang has been very difficult ever since then. No school will take him anymore. I'm his fourth governess—and I don't know whether I'm going to stay much longer."

"Why don't schools want him?" I asked.

"I don't know exactly," answered Aunt Matilda. "Nobody in the house talks about it. I got just a hint of it from the cook: He's supposed to have attacked some of his classmates and hurt them."

"Hurt them?"

"And on top of that, he supposedly said he was a werewolf—a person who turns into a wolf when the moon is full!"

Cold shivers ran up and down my spine. "Where is he now?" I asked.

"In his room, I hope." Suddenly she added, "Oh, if only I hadn't agreed to let you come here!"

With that she went to the door and turned the key.

That night I couldn't sleep, and it wasn't because of the sofa that Aunt Matilda had made up for me.

It was because I kept hearing long, drawn-out howls, as if a dog were in the house.

"Aunt Matilda, is there a dog here?" I called to my aunt, who was sleeping in the next room.

"No," she answered.

"Don't you hear a dog howling?"

"It's outside."

"No. A dog must be here, in the house."

"There is no dog," she said. "It's Wolf-gang."

"Wolfgang?" I echoed, aghast. "Why is he doing that?"

"I told you, he's moonstruck. He wants to go out into the garden."

"If he keeps on howling so loud, I won't be able to sleep!"

"Nor will I," said Aunt Matilda.

We were silent for a while.

After some time Aunt Matilda said, "It's never been as bad as tonight."

"Can't you tell him to stop?" I asked.

"I don't know. But maybe you're right—maybe he'll calm down if I talk to him nicely."

She got up. "But you're staying here!" she ordered.

"Alone?"

"Yes," she said firmly. "And lock the door behind me."

Then she went out. I ran to the door—but I didn't lock it. I was too anxious to see what would happen next.

A couple of minutes passed. Then suddenly the howling stopped. In the stillness my pulse was the loudest thing I heard.

If I hadn't been so curious, I would have turned the key right then and crept back under the covers. Instead I stood there, shivering with excitement, and waited.

First I heard faraway voices. They seemed to be arguing. Then a cry: "Don't!" and a sound like splintering glass.

In the chaos that followed, I heard a dull thud and a loud yell; then quick steps came down the stairs.

I quickly locked the door and jumped into

bed. The next minutes seemed to stretch endlessly. The only thing I could hear was the ticking of the clock. It was horrible! I thought any moment might be my last.

When there was a knock at the door, I jumped out of bed with a yell. But then I recognized my aunt's voice, and I ran to unlock the door.

She walked quickly to the table and turned on the floor lamp. She looked very pale and upset, but she was trying to hide it. She said very casually, "You can go to sleep now."

"Sleep?"

"Yes. Wolfgang won't bother us anymore tonight. And I'll stay awake to watch over you."

"But I can't sleep if you don't tell me what happened," I answered.

She went to the window and opened the curtains wide. "If I tell you, you *really* won't be able to sleep," she said softly, almost in a whisper.

"Tell me. Please!" I insisted.

With a jerk she pulled the curtains closed. "I'm going to give my notice," she said.

"Because of Wolfgang?" I asked.

She stayed by the window and didn't answer.

"I heard someone cry out," I said, to show her that I knew more than she thought. "And then splintering glass."

She turned around and looked at me. "It was so awful," she said tonelessly. "Blood everywhere . . ."

"Blood?" I repeated, horrified.

"Yes," she said, and then she told me what had happened.

Wolfgang had locked himself in his room. Aunt Matilda had knocked on his door and called, "Open up—it's me."

To her surprise he stopped howling and asked, "What do you want?" quite politely.

"I want to talk to you," she answered.

"Did my parents send you?"

"No."

He came to the door and opened it. His room was a dreadful mess—books and note-books lay on the floor, his underwear had been ripped from the closet, and Wolfgang was running back and forth like a caged animal.

"What do you want to talk about?" he cried.

His hair hung wildly over his forehead and covered his eyes.

"We can't sleep," said Aunt Matilda.

"Then let me out!"

"You know that I'm not allowed to do that. Your father has forbidden it."

At that moment Wolfgang's stepmother

came into the room, wearing a dressing gown.

"So you're quiet at last? Haven't you tormented us enough with your howling?" she asked in a hate-filled voice, looking around her in disgust. "But just you wait: Now we'll have some order in here! We'll start with your nails!"

And, in fact, she was holding a pair of sharp little scissors in her hand.

Wolfgang drew back and growled softly.

"Why don't you leave the boy alone?" Aunt Matilda said, trying to calm both of them down. "Tomorrow morning I'm sure he'll be willing to have his nails cut. Right, Wolfgang?"

He didn't answer. Instead he growled louder, more menacingly. His stepmother laughed shrilly.

"We'll soon see which of us has stronger

nerves!" she cried. "Now, give me your right hand."

She was standing only a step away from him.

Wolfgang's face was contorted with rage. He held his hands clasped firmly behind his back.

"Oh, you don't want to!" she mocked. "The sulky little boy again! Well, we'll see about getting rid of your sulks!"

These last words were spoken so hatefully, they chilled Aunt Matilda to the marrow.

"Don't!" she cried, but it was too late: Wolfgang lunged at his stepmother and scratched her face and neck. Then he raced toward the locked window. He broke the pane and jumped out—from the second floor!

"And then?" I cried.

"I don't know," said Aunt Matilda slowly. "He ran away. There was blood everywhere:

on the window seat, below on the terrace, on the garden path. . . . We looked for him, but he had disappeared."

She took a deep breath. Then she went on: "Tomorrow we're leaving. You can't stay here one day longer—and neither can I."

I was never to see Wolfgang again.

When Aunt Matilda and I left the house the next morning, he still hadn't come back. The only things they found were his clothes and shoes, which a servant had discovered in the maze under a hedge. They were covered with hanks of yellow-gray hair—wolf hair.

That afternoon I was at home again, accompanied by Aunt Matilda. For the next few weeks she took care of me, and we visited my mother in the hospital.

Freddy's mother finished.

"And Wolfgang?" Freddy asked.

His mother shrugged. "I never went back again."

"What about Aunt Matilda's things? Didn't she have to go and get them?"

"They came later in a moving van."

"Poor Wolfgang!" said Freddy. "He had nobody who cared about him!"

"Yes, life is unfair like that sometimes. But *you* don't have anything to complain about."

"That's what you think."

"Are you saying we don't care about you?"

"Well . . . I admit you *have* been telling me stories. . . ."

"Oh, come on!"

"Hey. I know a scary story that just fits," said Freddy.

"Fits what?"

"Fits that parents have to care about their children."

"Will you tell it to me?"

"Later—when it's finished."

"You mean you made it up yourself?"

"Yes."

"I can't wait to hear it," his mother said, laughing.

AND
THEY WENT
OVER THE HILL

Determined to have his scary story finished by dinnertime, Freddy spent the whole next day writing.

"Do you want to hear it?" he called to his parents, who were sitting in the living room.

"Of course!" "Gladly!" they answered, and came into his room, their faces filled with curiosity.

" 'It was a Friday in July,' " Freddy read out loud.

On the great meadow in the town park everything was ready. There was going to be a good-bye party for the kindergarten class.

Some of the parents had set up tables and chairs that afternoon—small ones for the

children, big ones for the adults. They had decorated the tables with blue paper table-cloths, blue napkins, and little ships and flags that the children had made. Hanging between the trees was a chain of colorful streamers, like those on cruise ships.

The party was to begin at six o'clock.

Shortly after six they were all there.

Every family had brought something, and the tables sagged under the weight of bottles, bowls, and plates.

On the children's table there were cupcakes, Gummy Bears, lollipops, cookies, wafers, candies, chocolates, peanuts, pretzels, and potato chips.

There was much more food than the eleven children could eat, although they stuffed themselves wildly. And they drank gallons of juice and soda.

After a while Jonah began to feel sick, and Anna and Marie took him into the bushes so he could throw up.

The grown-ups hadn't noticed anything. They were busy toasting each other. After all, it was their last party, and they wanted to celebrate one last time what a terrific bunch of parents they had been.

After the summer vacation the children

were going to be in different classes, and who knew whether they would ever all be together again?

The children were having eating contests with their cupcakes. But Sarah won every time, so after a while the others didn't feel like playing the game anymore.

Matthew took a cupcake and threw it at Nina. She yelled bloody murder and pulled the sticky mess out of her hair. Jonah had to throw up again, and this time Miriam went into the bushes with him.

Marie suggested they have a chocolate-eating contest. But the others said having eating contests all the time was boring, and they jumped up from their chairs.

The grown-ups had gotten up too. They stood together in little groups, eating and talking.

"Come on, let's have an egg race!" said Max.

He got a couple of spoons and a dish of hard-boiled eggs from the adults' table, but none of the children wanted to play.

So he began to aim the eggs at the streamers, and pretty soon the other children joined him.

Ulla, their teacher, went over to the children.

"Play something sensible for a change," she suggested.

"Like what?" asked Jacob.

"Other times you always have such good ideas," said Ulla.

"Why don't you grown-ups play with us?" asked Anna.

"Yes, that's right," Sarah agreed. "Last year you played kick the can and ran sack races with us."

"We think it's better for you children to make up your own games."

"You just want to get rid of us!" said Matthew.

Ulla laughed, embarrassed. "Of course we don't. . . . But do you know something? This is the last time that we'll be together, and we'd like to be able to talk among ourselves a little bit. . . ."

"Talk a little bit!" grumbled Miriam. "You've been talking the whole time!"

"I'm going to go ask them if they'll play kick the can with us!" Sarah said, and she ran over to the group where her mother was standing.

After a short time she came back, furious. "They don't want to! They say there are enough of us kids to play."

The children looked sullen.

Suddenly Ulla had an idea. "Why don't you go for a walk with your lanterns?" she asked. "It's already getting dark."

"Oh, yes," the children cried happily.

Ulla went and got the lanterns and lit the candles. The children had lined up and were talking in an excited babble of voices. Sarah had the prettiest lantern, a big sun. She stood at the head of the line. Matthew was the tail end, with a moon lantern.

The grown-ups watched and smiled.

"Don't you want to join us?" called Sarah.

"Join you? You're not babies anymore," her mother answered.

"But it's getting dark!" said Matthew.

"So what?" His father laughed.

Anna called, "We don't want to go alone. We're afraid of the dark."

The grown-ups laughed.

"And you say you're old enough to be going into first grade?" Nina's father said mockingly.

The children whispered together.

Then they were suddenly quiet, and the slow, solemn train began to move.

Their parents watched as they went farther and farther away, and spoke wistfully about the wonderful kindergarten days that were now coming to an end.

"They were such a good group!" said Anna's mother.

"And they really stuck together," said Miriam's father.

"And they always had such wild ideas," said Ulla.

Now the children were going up the little

hill in the middle of the town park. All you could see of their lanterns were small, bright dots.

"They look like will-o'-the-wisps!" said Anna's father.

The first lantern was just disappearing behind the hill, then the second. Finally they were all gone.

"Where are they going?" asked Jonah's mother.

"It must be a new game," answered Jacob's father. "We're probably supposed to look for them."

"Oh, I don't feel like it," Sarah's mother said.

"They'll come back when they get bored."

After half an hour the parents began to get nervous.

After three quarters of an hour they began to search.

At the bottom of the hill they found Jonah.

He had thrown up again and was so weak that he couldn't walk any farther. His lantern had gone out long ago.

"Where are the others?" cried Anna's mother.

"They went over the hill . . ." Jonah said dully.

The parents searched the whole town park, every nook and cranny—but they never found the ten children again!

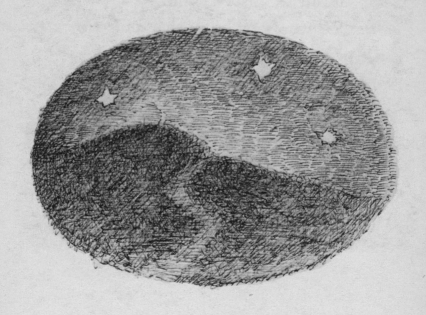

"That was really a scary story!" said Freddy's mother.

Freddy smiled, flattered. "Did you like it?"

"I thought it was a little exaggerated," said his father.

"How come?" asked Freddy indignantly.

"Do you really think there are parents who take so little care of their children and think only about themselves and their own pleasure? We were never like that while you were in kindergarten."

"You only think that because it was so long ago," replied Freddy. "Don't you remember how we had a party in the town park and Lena fell into the lake and would have drowned if we kids hadn't pulled her out? You grown-ups hadn't noticed a thing."

"Yes, that's true," his father admitted.

"And besides, with a scary story you're not

supposed to ask about the how and why," Freddy added, "or it loses its magic."

His parents looked at each other and laughed.

"You talk like a poet," his mother said. Then she asked, "Is it okay if I look at your notebook?"

His heart beating loudly, Freddy gave her the notebook. "FREDDY'S COLLECTED SCARY STORIES," she read out loud. "That sounds as if you plan to write more stories!"

Freddy nodded.

"I'm going to. Writing stories really helps when you're bored!"